The
Story Girl

Book 4

™

From the author of Anne of Green Gables

L.M. Montgomery

'The Story Girl
Book 4

DREAMS, SCHEMES, AND MYSTERIES

Adapted by Barbara Davoll

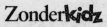

Zonderkidz

We want to hear from you. Please send your comments about this book to us in care of zreview@zondervan.com. Thank you.

Zonderkidz.

The children's group of Zondervan

www.zonderkidz.com

Dreams, Schemes, and Mysteries

© 2004 The Zondervan Corporation, David Macdonald, trustee and Ruth Macdonald

Requests for information should be addressed to:
Grand Rapids, Michigan 49530

Library of Congress Cataloging-in-Publication Data pending

ISBN: 0–310–706017

Editor: Gwen Ellis
Interior design: Susan Ambs
Art direction: Laura Maitner

04 05 06 07 /❖OP/ 10 9 8 7 6 5 4 3 2 1

Contents

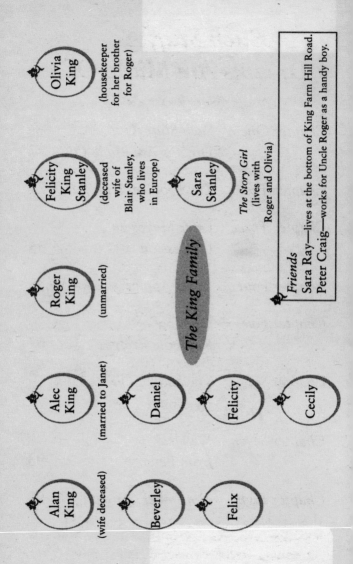

The King Family

Olivia King (housekeeper for her brother for Roger)

Felicity King Stanley (deceased wife of Blair Stanley, who lives in Europe)

Sara Stanley
The Story Girl
(lives with Roger and Olivia)

Roger King (unmarried)

Alec King (married to Janet)

Daniel

Felicity

Cecily

Alan King (wife deceased)

Beverley

Felix

Friends
Sara Ray—lives at the bottom of King Farm Hill Road.
Peter Craig—works for Uncle Roger as a handy boy.

Such Stuff As Dreams Are Made Of

For a week we ate unlawful bedtime snacks
and dreamed dreams as wild as we wanted.
Our digestions went out of order and our tempers too. The Story Girl and I had a fight—
something that had never happened before.

Chapter One

The glorious summer on Prince Edward Island was drawing to a close. All of us King cousins—particularly my brother, Felix, and I—were sad to see it ending. Soon Felix and I would have to go back to Toronto to rejoin our father. We could hardly bear the thought of leaving our cousins and the Island that we had come to love. In the last few days, all of us cousins were writing our dreams down for a fun memory of the summer and fall spent there together.

One evening Peter, Dan, and I were on our way to the King orchard with our dream books tucked under our arms. As we walked along, Peter told us that he needed our advice. Knowing that all of our girl cousins were waiting for us, we went around by the way of the woods, so they wouldn't see us. They were always curious as cats whenever we had something private to talk about. When we got into the woods, Peter told us about his problem.

"Last night I dreamed I was in church," he said.

"It was full of people, and I walked up the aisle to the King pew and sat down. Then I realized that I hadn't a stitch of clothes on. Not one blessed stitch! Now," Peter dropped his voice, "what is bothering me is this: Would it be proper to tell a dream like that in front of the girls? I know we all agreed to tell each other our dreams, but what about this one?" he asked with a worried look.

I was of the opinion that he shouldn't tell it, but Dan said he didn't see why not. He said he'd tell it as quick as any other dream and that there was nothing bad in it.

"But the girls are your own relatives," said Peter. "They're no relation to me, and that makes a difference. Besides, they're all so ladylike. I guess I'd better not risk it. I'm pretty sure Aunt Jane wouldn't think it was proper to tell such a dream. And I don't want to offend Felic—any of them." Peter had almost said "Felicity" but caught himself just in time, as if the rest of us didn't know that he had a wild crush on her.

So Peter never told that dream, nor did he write it down. But I remember what he did write in his dream book for the date of September 15. "Last nite i dremed a drem. it wasn't a polit drem so i won't rite it down."

The girls saw his dream book, but they never tried to find out what the "drem" was. They really

10

were decent and perfect "ladies" in the truest sense of the word. Although they were full of fun and mischief, no vulgar word was ever uttered by any of them or us boys in front of them. If we had been guilty of filthy talk, Cecily's face would have turned blood red, Felicity's sharp tongue would have lashed strong enough to shrivel us.

I remember one time Dan swore. Uncle Alec whipped him for it—the only time he ever punished any of his children that way. Dan was filled with sorrow and repented quickly, because Cecily cried all night over his sin. The next day, he promised her that he would never swear again, and he kept his word.

About that time, the Story Girl and Peter began to dream dreams that were far more exciting than any of ours. Their dreams were so colorful that it was hard for the rest of us to believe they weren't making them up. But the Story Girl was a soul of honor. And Peter, early in life, had his feet set in the path of truthfulness by his Aunt Jane. Neither of them had ever been known to lie.

When they assured us seriously that their dreams happened exactly as they described them, what else could we believe? But we felt sure there had to be something going on—some reason for their exciting dreams. For two weeks they dreamed the most fantastic dreams. We were amazed and curious. What was their dream secret? There was no finding out from the Story Girl. She kept secrets better than anyone. We didn't dare tease her about it, because the whole two weeks she claimed she wasn't feeling well.

We overheard Aunt Olivia and Aunt Janet talking about it.

"I don't know what's wrong with the child," said Aunt Olivia. "She hasn't seemed like herself the past two weeks. She complains of a headache and has no appetite. And I don't like her color. I'm about ready to take her to the doctor."

"Give her a good dose of medicinal tea first," said Aunt Janet. "I've been saved from many doctor's bills in my family by using medicinal tea." But the medicinal tea made no difference. The Story Girl kept on dreaming and so did Peter.

"If we can't figure out what's making the two of them dream such exciting dreams, none of us has a chance of winning the dream contest."

Finally Felicity solved the mystery for us. She threatened never to speak to Peter again if he didn't tell her their "dream" secret. She promised him that if he told her why their dreams were so colorful, she would let him walk beside her to Sunday school all the rest of the summer, and he could carry her books. Peter couldn't resist telling her that he and the Story Girl had been dreaming wild dreams because they had been eating rich, indigestible things just before bed. During the day, Sara Stanley would smuggle tidbits from the pantry for herself and Peter. They would save them to eat just before bed. The result was wild dreams. It also accounted for the Story Girl's sickness.

After the secret was out, the Story Girl was very frank about it all. "I knew Felicity would get it out of Peter sometime. Last night I ate a piece of mincemeat pie, a lot of pickles, and two grape jelly tarts. I guess I overdid it because I got real sick and couldn't sleep at all. So, of course I didn't have any dreams. I guess I should have stopped with the pie and pickles.

"Peter only had pie and pickles, and he had an elegant dream. He dreamed the old woman, Peg Bowen, caught him and put him to boil alive in that big black pot that hangs outside her door. He woke up before the water got hot though.

"Well, Miss Felicity, now you'll have to follow through with your promise to Peter," said the Story Girl. "How will you like it, walking to Sunday school with a *hired boy* in his patched trousers?"

"I won't have to," said Felicity happily. "Peter is having a new suit made. It's to be ready by Saturday. I knew that before I promised."

The Story Girl turned away from her in disgust. Felicity was just being Felicity, but the Story Girl despised it when she talked about Peter like he was second-class. Felicity held this opinion because he was Uncle Roger's hired boy. Sometimes she was so snobby we could hardly stand her.

Now that we knew how to produce exciting dreams, we all followed the example of Peter and the Story Girl.

"There is no chance for me to have any horrid dreams," said Sara Ray sadly. "Ma won't let me have anything at all to eat before I go to bed. I don't think it's fair."

"Can't you hide something away through the day as we do?" asked Felicity.

"No, Ma always keeps the pantry locked, so the hired girl won't steal from us."

For a week we ate unlawful bedtime snacks and dreamed dreams as wild as we wanted. Our digestions went out of order and our tempers too. The Story Girl and I had a fight—something that had never happened before. Only Peter was his same old self. Nothing could upset his stomach.

One night the grown-ups were away for the evening. They were attending a lecture at Markdale, so we ate our snacks openly, without anyone stopping us. Cecily came into the pantry with a large cucumber. She ate the whole thing. I remember eating a solid hunk of pork fat and a slab of cold plum pudding.

"I thought you didn't like cucumbers, Cecily," Dan remarked.

"I don't," answered Cecily, making a face. "But Peter says they're splendid for dreaming. He ate one that night he had the dream about being caught by cannibals. I'd eat three cucumbers if I could dream a dream like that."

We had just finished our snacks when we heard the wheels of Uncle Alec's buggy coming over the bridge in the hollow. Felicity quickly put all the evidence away, and we were in our beds when they came in. Soon the house was dark and silent. I was just dropping off to sleep when I heard a commotion in the girls' room across the hall.

Through our open door, I saw a white-clad figure flit down the hall to Aunt Janet's room. From the girls' room came moans and cries.

"Cecily's sick," said Dan, springing out of bed. "That cucumber must have disagreed with her."

In a few minutes, the whole household was awake. Cecily was very, very sick. Much sicker than Dan had been when he had eaten the bad berries. Uncle Alec went for the doctor. Aunt Janet tried every home remedy she could think of, but nothing stopped the awful pain and cramping. Felicity told Aunt Janet about the cucumber, but Aunt Janet didn't think it could have made her so sick.

"But she ate a really big one, Mother," said Felicity, wringing her hands as Cecily moaned and tossed like she might die.

"What on earth for?" asked Aunt Janet. "I didn't think she even liked them."

"She doesn't," said Felicity. "It was that wretched Peter. He told her it would make her dream better."

"Dream? Why did she want to dream?" questioned our aunt, who was terribly upset.

"Oh, to have something worthwhile to write in her dream book. We all have dream books, you know, and we've been eating rich things to make us dream. But if Cecily . . . oh, I'll never forgive myself," she sobbed.

Just then the doctor came, but he couldn't seem to help Cecily. Like Aunt Janet, he declared that cucumbers couldn't make her so ill. Then he found out that she had drunk a glass of milk too. Then the mystery was solved.

"We're not sure, but we think milk and cucumber eaten together make a bad poison," he said. "No wonder the child is sick. It won't kill her, but she'll be pretty miserable for two or three days."

She was miserable. And we were too. Aunt Janet investigated the whole affair, and the matter of our dream books was discussed in a family meeting. I don't know which hurt our feelings more, the scolding we got from Aunt Janet or the ridicule and teasing Uncle Roger gave us. Peter got it worse than any of us.

"I didn't tell Cecily to drink the milk, and the cucumber alone wouldn't have hurt her," he grumbled. Cecily was able to be up by then, so Peter thought it was alright to grumble a bit. "Besides, she begged me to tell her what would be good for dreams. I just told her as a favor. And now your aunt Janet blames me for it all."

"And Aunt Janet says that after this we are never to have anything to eat before we go to bed except plain bread and milk," said Felix sadly.

"They'd like to stop us from dreaming altogether," said the Story Girl.

"We needn't worry about the bread-and-milk rule," added Felicity. "Ma made a rule like that once before and kept it for a week. Then we just slipped back into the old way. That will happen this time too. But of course we won't be able to get any more rich foods before bed, and our dreams will be pretty boring after this."

"Well, let's go down to the Pulpit Stone, and I'll tell you a story I know," said the Story Girl.

We went—and in a short time we were laughing. We had already forgotten the wrongs of our cruel grown-ups.

Soon we heard the grown-ups come into the orchard. They were all laughing as they joined our circle. They sometimes did this when they finished their work. We liked our grown-ups the best at those times, for then they seemed like children again.

Uncle Roger and Uncle Alec lolled in the grass like boys. Aunt Olivia looked like a pretty flower in her prettiest print dress—a delightful pale purple. She had a knot of yellow ribbon at her throat and sat with her arm about Cecily, as she smiled sweetly at the rest of us. Even Aunt Janet's motherly face lost its everyday look of anxious care.

The Story Girl was in high spirits that night. Her stories had never sparkled with such wit and fun.

"Sara Stanley," said Aunt Olivia, shaking her finger at her after she told a funny story, "you'll be famous someday."

As we left the orchard, I walked along behind Uncle Roger and Aunt Olivia.

"That girl has a lot of talent," said Uncle Roger.

"I know, Roger," answered Aunt Olivia. "I wonder what is in store for her?"

"Fame," he responded. "If she ever has a chance, that is. I suppose her father will see to that. At least I hope he will. You and I never had our chance, Olivia. I hope Sara will have hers."

That was the first time I began to understand that Uncle Roger and Aunt Olivia had both cherished dreams and ambitions in their youth, but those dreams had never been fulfilled.

"Someday, Olivia," Uncle Roger went on, "you and I may find that we are the aunt and uncle of a great actress. If a girl of fourteen can make her family believe for ten minutes that she is a snake, what will she be able to do when she's thirty!"

When he realized I was behind him, he dismissed me, saying, "Run along to bed, Bev, and don't be eating any cucumbers before you go."

Grown-ups are like elephants. They never forget.

The Problem with Pat

We had been pretty brave until then, but our strained nerves gave way to sheer panic. Peter gave a little yelp of pure terror. We turned and ran across the clearing and into the woods.

Chapter Two

All of us King cousins were down in the dumps, and even the grown-ups took an interest in our trouble. The Story Girl's cat, Paddy, our own dear precious Pat, as we sometimes called him, was sick—very, very sick.

On Friday, he moped and refused his saucer of new milk at milking time. The next morning, he stretched himself on the platform outside Uncle Roger's back door, laid his head on his black paws, and refused to take any notice of anything or anybody. Only when the Story Girl stroked him did he give one sad little mew, as if to ask why we didn't do something to help him.

At that Cecily and Felicity and Sara Ray all began crying, and we boys felt choked up. I caught Peter behind Aunt Olivia's dairy later in the day. If ever a boy had been crying, it was Peter. He didn't deny it either, but he wouldn't own up to it that he was crying about Paddy. "Nonsense!" he answered.

"What were you crying for then?" I asked.

"I'm crying because . . . because my Aunt Jane is dead," he said defiantly.

"But your Aunt Jane died two years ago," I said skeptically.

"Well, I've had to do without her for two years now, and that's worse than if it had just happened."

"I believe you were crying because Pat is so sick," I said firmly.

"As if I'd cry about a cat!" he scoffed and marched off whistling.

We tried the lard and powder treatment, smearing Pat's paws and sides liberally. It usually worked, as Pat always licked and cleaned himself and would get the medicine when he did. But Pat made no effort to lick it off this time.

"I tell you he's a mighty sick cat," said Peter darkly. "When a cat don't care what he looks like, he's pretty far gone."

"If only we knew what was the matter with him, we might do something," said the Story Girl. She was nearer tears and sadder than I'd ever seen her. She sat on the floor, gently stroking her poor pet's unresponsive head.

"I could tell you what's the matter with him, but you'd only laugh at me," said Peter.

We all looked at him.

"Peter Craig, what do you mean?" asked Felicity.

"'Zackly what I say."

"Then, if you know what's the matter with Paddy, tell us," commanded the Story Girl, standing up. She said it quietly, but Peter obeyed. I think he would have obeyed if she, in that tone and with those eyes, had ordered him to jump off a bridge. I know I would have.

"I think that old woman, Peg Bowen, made him sick," Peter said defiantly.

"What? How could she make him sick?" asked Story Girl.

"There now! I said you wouldn't believe me. I think she poisoned him."

The Story Girl looked at Peter, at the rest of us, and then at poor Pat. "Do you really think she could have poisoned him?" asked the Story Girl.

"Well, I don't know for sure. But he's sick enough to die, and he was fine yesterday."

"Why would she want to poison Pat?" asked Cecily.

"I'll tell you why," said Peter. "Thursday afternoon when you were all in school, Peg Bowen came here. Your Aunt Olivia gave her a good lunch."

"Peg Bowen is not our favorite person, but Aunt Olivia is good to every poor person and so is Mother," said Felicity. "We are careful not to offend Peg because she is spiteful. Once she set fire to a man's barn in Markdale when he offended her."

"All right. But wait till I tell you. When Peg Bowen was leaving, Pat was all stretched out on the steps. She tramped on his tail. You know Pat doesn't like to have his tail meddled with. He turned himself around and clawed her bare foot. If you'd seen the look she gave him, you'd think she hated him. She was furious. I wouldn't put it past her to poison him," Peter said sadly. "Paddy got sick the morning after she was here."

We looked at each other in a miserable silence.

"If that's so, though I don't believe it, we can't do anything," said the Story Girl sadly. "Pat will die."

Cecily and Sara Ray began to cry again.

"I'd do anything to save Pat's life," cried Cecily.

"There's nothing we can do," said Felicity impatiently.

"I suppose," sobbed Cecily, "we might go to Peg Bowen and ask if she could make Pat better. You know a lot of people believe she has healing powers. She grows all those herbs that are supposed to make people better. She might help Pat if we ask her."

At first we were shocked by her suggestion. To go to Peg Bowen—to seek her out in her mysterious woodland home—was not an option. The thought scared us to death. We were surprised that this suggestion should come from timid Cecily, of all people! But then, there was poor Pat! If something could be done for him, we would do it.

"Do you suppose it would do any good?" asked the Story Girl desperately. "Even if she did make Pat sick, I suppose it would only make her more cross if we went and accused her of poisoning him. We wouldn't have to accuse her, though."

"We should take her some presents to soften her up toward us," said Cecily wisely.

"Good idea!" agreed the Story Girl. "We must write the letter and take the presents right away before it gets dark."

I ripped a page out of my dream book and handed it to her. "How shall I begin it?" she asked. "It would never do to say, 'Dear Peg.' And 'Miss Bowen' sounds ridiculous."

"Besides, nobody knows whether she's Miss Bowen or not," said Felicity. "She grew up in Boston, and some say she was married there. They say her husband left her, and that's when she got funny in the head. If she's married, she won't like being called 'Miss.'"

Peter came to the rescue with a practical suggestion.

"How about 'Respected Madam'?" he suggested. "Aunt Jane got a letter once from a school director who wrote to her. That's how he began it."

The Story Girl wrote:

Respected Madam,

We want to ask a very great favor of you, and we hope you will kindly grant it if you can. Our

favorite cat, Paddy, is very sick, and we are afraid he is going to die. Do you think you could cure him? And will you please try? We are all so fond of him, and he is such a good cat and has no bad habits.

Of course, if any of us tramps on his tail, he will scratch us, but you know a cat can't bear to have his tail tramped on. It's a very tender part of him. He wouldn't mean any harm by it.

If you can cure Paddy for us, we will always be very, very grateful to you. These small gifts are to show our gratitude, if you can help our dear Paddy.

Very respectfully yours,

Sara Stanley

"I think it has a very fine sound," observed Peter after she read the letter to us.

"I think it's too fine," criticized Felicity. "I doubt if she'll understand it all."

After consideration we decided the letter was all right and gathering our gifts, we started on our way to her house. Sara Ray volunteered to stay with Pat while we were gone. We didn't see any reason to tell the grown-ups about our errand. Grown-ups have such peculiar views sometimes. They might have forbidden us to go, or worse yet, they might have laughed at us.

Peg Bowen's house was nearly a mile away, even by the shortcut past the swamp and up the wooded hill. We went down through the brook meadow and over the little plank bridge in the hollow. When we reached the green gloom of the woods beyond, we began to feel frightened. None of us would admit it though. We walked very close together and no one spoke. We wanted to be careful. We knew the old woman might be hiding behind some tree, listening to us.

Finally we came to the lane that led to her house. We were all very pale then, and our hearts were pounding. The red September sun hung low between the tall spruces. Everything looked red and weird. Just beyond a sudden bend in the lane was Peg's house. It was a small, shaky building with a sagging roof, surrounded by a jungle of weeds. The oddest thing about it was that there was no entrance on the ground floor as in most houses. The only door was in the upper story, which was reached by a flight of rickety steps. There was no sign of life except a large black cat sitting on the top step.

In a tense, breathless silence, the Story Girl placed our gifts on the lowest step and laid her letter on top of the pile. Her fingers trembled and her face was pale.

Suddenly the door above us opened, and Peg Bowen herself appeared. She was a tall, skinny old woman wearing a short ragged skirt that didn't reach her knees. She had on a red print blouse and a man's hat. Her feet, arms, and neck were bare; and she had an old clay pipe in her mouth. Her brown face was lined with a hundred wrinkles, and long tangled hair fell to her shoulders. She was scowling, and her flashing black eyes were not friendly.

We had been pretty brave until then, but our strained nerves gave way to sheer panic. Peter gave a little yelp of pure terror. We turned and ran across the clearing and into the woods. We tore off like mad, hunted creatures, believing she was after us. Our flight was wilder than anything we had written about in our dream books.

The Story Girl was in front of me, and I remember the huge jumps she made over fallen logs and bushes. Cecily kept gasping behind me, "Oh, Bev, hurry, hurry!"

We didn't stop until we were finally in the brook meadow. The sky was a dainty shell pink, and lazy cows were in the pasture around us. We had a glad realization that we were back home and that Peg Bowen had not caught us.

"Oh, wasn't that an awful experience?" gasped Cecily, shuddering.

"It come on me so sudden," said Peter in a shamed voice. "If I'd a knowed she was a-goin' to pop out like that, I coulda stood my ground. But when she came out so sudden like, I thought I was done for."

When we got home and found Pat was no better, we were all sure the end was near for the poor old cat.

"Well, Pat won't die alone," declared the Story Girl. "I'm going to take him into the kitchen and sit up with him all night."

We didn't think Aunt Olivia would allow that, but she did. She was really a great little aunt. Aunt Janet, of course, would not allow the rest of us to stay up, as Pat wasn't our own cat. As the five of us trudged up the stairs to bed, our hearts were just sick.

"There's nothing we can do now except pray to God to make Pat better," said Cecily.

I must say, she said it as though it were the last resort.

"I don't believe it would be right to pray about a cat," remarked Felicity.

"I don't see why not," retorted Cecily. "God made Paddy just as much as he made you, Felicity King. And I'm sure he's more able to help him than Peg Bowen. Anyhow, I'm going to pray for Pat with all my might, and I'd like to see you try and stop me. Of course, I won't mix it up with more important things. I'll just tack it on after I've finished asking the blessings but before I say amen."

More prayers than Cecily's were offered up to the Lord that night on behalf of Paddy. I distinctly

31

heard Felix (who always said his prayers out loud) pray, "Oh God, please make Pat better by morning. *Please* do."

And I am not the least bit ashamed to confess that when I knelt down to say my prayers, I prayed hard for his healing. Then I went to sleep, comforted by the simple thought that my good heavenly Father would, after taking care of "important things," remember poor Pat.

As soon as we were up the next morning, we rushed off to Uncle Roger's. We met Peter and the Story Girl in the lane, and the moment we saw their happy faces, we knew they had good news.

"Pat's better," cried the Story Girl triumphantly. "Last night around midnight, he began to lick his paws. Then he licked himself all over and went to sleep on the sofa. When I awoke this morning, he was washing his face, and he has taken a whole saucer of milk."

"I guess Cecily's prayer had more to do with Pat's getting better than Peg Bowen," said Felicity.

"I'm going to believe that it was the praying," said Cecily decidedly. "It's much better to believe that God, rather than Peg Bowen, cured Pat."

"Mind you, I ain't saying God couldn't cure Pat. But nobody can make me believe that Peg Bowen wasn't behind him being sick," asserted Peter.

"Maybe so," said the Story Girl. "But we all prayed powerfully hard. It just proves to me that prayer works. All I know is, Pat is better, and I am thankful to God that he is."

And that ended the discussion.

Peter Makes an Impression

An electric shock seemed to run through
all of us listening. Everyone suddenly
looked alert. Peter had, in one sentence,
done what my whole sermon had failed
to do. He had made an impression.

Chapter Three

One warm Sunday evening in early autumn, we all—grown-ups and children—were sitting in the orchard by the Pulpit Stone, singing some sweet old gospel hymns. Except for Sara Ray, we could all sing pretty well. She couldn't sing a note. Poor thing.

I remember it all just as if it were yesterday. I can see Uncle Alec's tired, brilliant blue eyes. I can see Aunt Janet's motherly face and Uncle Roger's blond beard and red cheeks and, oh yes, Aunt Olivia's beautiful form. The best singers were Cecily, with her sweet and silvery voice, and Uncle Alec, a fine tenor. There was a saying, "If you're a King, you sing." And sing we did.

That evening after we were all sung out, the grown-ups began to talk about their youth and the things they had done. It was always fun for us to hear them tell about when they were children. Now they were all prim and proper; but it seems that in their younger days, they had plenty of mischief, quarrels, and upsets.

The dusk crept into the orchard like a quiet angel. You could see her ... feel her ... hear her. She tiptoed softly from tree to tree, ever drawing nearer. Presently her filmy wings hovered over us, and through them gleamed the early stars of the autumn night.

The grown-ups got up and strolled away, unwilling to disturb the magical moment. We children stayed for a moment to talk over an idea the Story Girl had—a good idea we thought, one that promised to add some spice to life.

"I've thought of a splendid plan," she said. "It flashed into my mind when the uncles were talking about Uncle Edward. The beauty of it is that we can play it on Sundays. You know there are so few things we are allowed to do on Sundays, but this is a Christian game, so it will be all right."

"It isn't like the religious fruit basket game, is it?" asked Cecily anxiously. This was a game that hadn't worked out for us because of Peter. He couldn't play because he didn't know the Scriptures very well.

"No, this isn't a game at all," said the Story Girl. "It is this: Each of you boys must preach a sermon like Uncle Edward used to. Each of you choose a Sunday to preach, and we girls will judge which sermon is best and give you a prize. I'll give that picture that Father sent me last week."

The picture was a famous artist's picture of a fine deer. We boys were pleased and agreed. It was decided that I would be the first one to preach. I lay awake for an hour that night, thinking about what Scripture text I should use for the following Sunday. After tea the next day, I went to the barn and sat on a bale of hay, writing what I hoped would be a masterpiece of a sermon.

I decided to preach on missions. Using words, I painted a terrible picture of the dark, awful life of the poor heathen who bowed down to gods of wood and stone. God's who could never help them. Each time I had an important point to make, I wrote the word "thump" in red ink, so I'd be sure to thump the pulpit to emphasize the point.

I still have that sermon with all its unfaded red "thumps." It is filed away with my dream book. I'm not as proud of it as I once was. At the time, I didn't think Felix could beat it. And I certainly didn't think Dan had a chance—he wasn't even religious. As for Peter, I didn't suppose a boy who had hardly gone to church in his life could even be in the running to compete with me. He had so little education, and I came from a family with a real minister in it. Surely, I thought, I had the best chance of all to win that picture.

I wanted to memorize my sermon, so I preached it over and over with only Paddy sitting in the audience in the barn, patiently listening.

When we went to church the next Sunday, Reverend Marwood, the pastor, had at least three interested listeners. Felix, Peter, and I were taking mental notes on the art of preaching. Not a motion or a word escaped us. To be sure, none of us could even remember the text when we got home. But we knew just how to throw our heads back and clutch the edges of the pulpit when we announced it.

In the afternoon we all went to the orchard with our Bibles and hymnbooks in hand. I went up the stone steps of the Pulpit Stone, feeling rather nervous. My audience sat down gravely on the grass in front of me. We began with singing and the reading of the Scripture. We had agreed to omit the prayer, as that seemed too serious for playacting. But we took up a collection for missions. Dan passed one of Felicity's rosebud plates, and everyone put in a penny.

Before I was halfway through my sermon, I realized that it was horrible. It seemed to me that I preached it well enough. I didn't forget one thump. But my audience was plainly bored. When I stepped down from the pulpit, I felt I had failed to make any impression at all. Felix would be sure to get the prize.

"That was a very good sermon for a first attempt," the Story Girl said graciously. "It sounded just like real sermons I have heard."

At first she made me feel that I had not done so badly after all. But the other girls weighed in with their comments and my hopes were dashed.

"Every word of it was true," said Cecily, as though trying to say something good about it.

"I often feel," said Felicity in her prim, stuck-up way, "that we don't think enough about the heathen. Your sermon made me at least *think* about them."

Sara Ray really put me in my place. "I liked it 'cause it was nice and short," she said.

Later I asked Dan what he thought of it. Since he had decided not to compete, I thought I could depend on him for the truth.

"It was too much like a regular sermon to be interesting," said Dan frankly.

"I'd think that's what it should have been," I replied.

"Not if you wanted to make an impression," said Dan seriously. "You needed to have something different for that. Now Peter, he'll have something different."

"I don't think Peter can preach a sermon. He's hardly even gone to church," I replied.

"Maybe not," Dan answered, "but you'll see. He'll make an impression."

Peter's turn came next. He didn't write his sermon out. "That's too much hard work," he said.

"And I ain't choosing a text or a special Scripture verse for the whole sermon."

"Whoever heard of a sermon without a text?" asked Felix.

"I'm going to have a subject instead of a text. It will have three headings. You didn't have a single heading, Bev," he said to me. "If you have headings, you won't wander all over the Bible. You'll be more organized."

I was sorry I hadn't had headings and figured I would have made more of an impression if I had used some. "How's one to know about headings?" I asked.

"Well, I'm going to have them," said Peter.

"What are you going to preach on?" asked Felix.

"You'll find out next Sunday," Peter said, and that was all he would say.

The next Sunday was the first of October—a lovely day, as warm as June. We sat around the Pulpit Stone and waited for Peter. It was his Sunday off, and he had gone home the night before, but he said he'd be back for sure to preach his sermon. Soon he arrived. I felt right away that he had the advantage over me because he looked so handsome in his new navy blue suit, white collar, and bow tie. His black eyes shone and his curls were brushed up so that he sure looked the part of a minister.

Sara Ray was late but we decided to go ahead. We never knew for sure when she was coming. Sometimes her mother would change her plans at the last minute.

Peter chose the hymn we would sing and read the chapter of Scripture as if he'd been doing it all of his life. Reverend Marwood himself couldn't have done better.

"We will sing the hymn, omitting the fourth stanza," Peter said.

That was a fine touch that I had not thought of. I began to think Peter might have a chance to win after all.

When Peter was ready to begin, he put his hands in his pockets—something not usually done by ministers—and plunged in. He spoke in a conversational tone. He didn't put on a minister voice. He made his sermon very believable. There was no one writing it down, but I could have preached it again, word for word. And so could everyone else who heard it. It was an unforgettable sermon.

"Dearly beloved," said Peter, "my sermon is about the bad place—in short—hell."

An electric shock seemed to run through all of us listening. Everyone suddenly looked alert. Peter had in one sentence done what my whole sermon had failed to do. He had made an impression.

43

"I shall divide my sermon into three headings," continued Peter. "The first heading is 'What you must not do if you don't want to go to the bad place.' The second heading is 'What the bad place is like,' and the third heading is 'How to keep from going there.'

"Now there's a great many things you must not do, and it's very important to know what they are. You ought not to lose time in finding out. In the first place, you must never forget to mind what grownup people tell you—that is, *good* grown-up people."

"But how are you going to tell who the good grown-ups are?" asked Felix right out loud, forgetting he was in "church."

"Oh, that's easy," said Peter. "You can always just feel who is good and who isn't. And you mustn't tell lies, and you mustn't murder anyone. You must be 'specially careful to say your prayers and read the Bible and do what it says. And you shouldn't quarrel with your sister."

At this Felicity gave Dan a poke in the ribs, and Dan was up in arms at once.

"Don't you be preaching at me, Peter Craig," he cried out. "I won't stand for it. I don't quarrel with my sister any more than she quarrels with me. You can just leave me alone!"

"Who's touching you?" demanded Peter. "I didn't mention any names. A minister can say any-

44

thing he likes in the pulpit, as long as he doesn't mention any names, and nobody can answer back."

"All right, but you just wait till tomorrow," growled Dan.

"You mustn't play any weekday games on Sunday," Peter went on, "and you mustn't laugh in church. I did that once and I was awful sorry. And you mustn't pay attention to Paddy during family prayers, not even if he climbs up on your back and scratches you. And you mustn't call names or make faces."

"Amen," cried Felix, who had suffered many things because Felicity so often made faces at him.

Peter stopped and glared at him over the edge of the Pulpit Stone.

"You shouldn't call out like that right in the middle of a sermon," he scolded Felix.

"They do it all the time in the Methodist church at Markdale," argued Felix. "I've heard them."

"I know they do. That's the Methodist way, and it is all right for them. I haven't a word to say against the Methodists. My Aunt Jane was one, and I might have been one myself if I hadn't been so scared of Judgment Day. But you ain't Methodist. You're a Presbyterian, ain't you?"

"Yes, my whole family is."

"Very well then. You need to do things the Presbyterian way. Don't let me hear any more amens or I'll amen you!"

"Oh, please let him get on with his sermon. Nobody interrupted Beverley last Sunday," said the Story Girl.

"Bev didn't get up there and preach at us like that," muttered Dan.

"You mustn't fight," resumed Peter. "Of course, there are many other things you mustn't do, but these I've named are the most important. I'm not saying you'll go to the bad place for sure if you do them. I'm only saying that you're running a risk. The devil is looking for people who do these things, and he's more likely to trap you and send you to the bad place if you do them."

At this point Sara Ray arrived somewhat out of breath. Peter was annoyed and looked it.

"Sara Ray, you should have been here if you're one of the judges. You've missed the whole first heading of my sermon. One time when old Reverend Scott was preaching, a man came in late. Mr. Scott stopped till the man got seated and said, 'Friend, I hope you won't be late for heaven. To be *sure* you won't, I'll just start over.'

"And he did. He preached the whole sermon over. They said that gentleman was never late again."

"Let's not hear your first part again, Peter. Just go on now from where you were," encouraged the Story Girl.

Peter grabbed both sides of the Pulpit Stone and began preaching again. "I've come now to the second heading for my sermon—'What the bad place is like.'"

His description of the bad place was really hot. Later we found out that he had studied about it a lot. Peter had been reading the Bible steadily ever since "Judgment Sunday," when we all got scared out of our wits that the end of the world was coming. None of the rest of us had read the Bible through completely, and we sat openmouthed as he described the torments and flames and how long eternity was.

Suddenly Sara Ray sprang to her feet with a scream that changed into strange laughter. We all stared at her in shock, including Peter. We realized that she was having a fit of hysterics.

"She's gone crazy," said Peter, coming down from the pulpit with a very pale face.

"You've frightened her with your dreadful sermon," said Felicity, hovering near and trying to console her.

She and Cecily took Sara by the arm and led her up to the house, still sobbing and crying as she went.

"I think you've made too much of an impression, Peter," said the Story Girl miserably.

"She needn't have got so scared," Peter replied. "If she had only waited until the third heading of my sermon, I'd have showed her how easy it is to go to heaven instead of the bad place. All you have to do is believe in Jesus. But you girls are always in such a hurry."

"Uh oh, look out. Here comes Uncle Alec," whispered my brother. "You're in for it now."

We had never seen Uncle Alec so angry. His blue eyes blazed as he said, "What have you been doing to frighten Sara Ray into such a condition?"

"We . . . we . . . were just having a preaching contest," explained the Story Girl. "And Peter preached about the bad place and it frightened her. That's all, Uncle Alec."

"All! I don't know what the result will be with that nervous, delicate child. She is shrieking in there, and nothing will quiet her. What do you mean by playing such a game on Sunday and making a joke of such things?"

"It wasn't a joke, Uncle Alec. It was all true from the Bible, and we weren't making a joke. We—"

"That's enough," interrupted Uncle Alec firmly. "Not one more word. Shame on you for making a joke of sacred things. Don't let me catch you doing such things on Sunday ever again."

There was no more to be said. As we walked to the house, Felix said in despair, "I'll never understand grown-ups. When Uncle Edward preached sermons, it was all right; but when we do it, they say we're 'making a joke of sacred things.'"

"It's no wonder we can't understand the grown-ups," said the Story Girl, "because we've never been grown-up ourselves. But they have been children, and I don't see why *they* can't understand *us*. Maybe we shouldn't have had the contest on Sundays. But all the same, I think Uncle Alec's mean to be so cross. Oh, I do hope poor Sara is all right."

Poor Sara was fine the next day, and she humbly begged Peter's pardon for disturbing his sermon. Peter granted it, but he did so quite grumpily because we were not allowed to finish the preaching contest. I don't think he ever really forgave Sara for keeping him from winning the prize painting.

"If we only hadn't had those crybaby girls mixed up in it all," grumped Felix. "We would still be having the contest. Cecily was as scared as Sara Ray. She just didn't show it as much."

"Well, you ought to be able to hear some real truth from the Bible, even if it is scary," was Peter's comment.

"Sara Ray couldn't help it," said the Story Girl. "It's just that she's very sensitive.

"We sure have had bad luck with all of our schemes lately. Like the dream books. Who'd ever have thought that Cecily would get so sick from cucumbers and milk? And now Sara having hysterics.

"I have an idea for a new game, but I'm almost afraid to mention it. I suppose something dreadful will come of it too."

"Oh, tell us what it is," everybody begged.

"Well, the idea is to eat one of the bitter apples from the bitter apple tree in the orchard without making a face."

Dan made a face to begin with. "I don't believe any of us can do that."

"*You* can't . . . that's for sure. You'd have to take huge bites to fill *your* big mouth," laughed Felicity.

"Well, *you* can't make your face any worse, Felicity, no matter what you eat," he snapped.

The brother and sister were at each other again. But then my brother, Felix, got into it too.

"Felicity makes faces when there's nothing to make faces at," said Felix, who had never liked her since she had said he was fat.

"I think the bitter apples would be real good for Felix," blasted Felicity. "They say sour things make fat people thin."

"Let's go and get the bitter apples," said Cecily, as Felix made a nasty face at Felicity.

We went to the bitter apple tree and each of us got an apple. The game was that everyone had to take a bite, chew it up, and swallow it, without making a face. Peter distinguished himself again. He crunched up the whole apple without changing his face in the slightest.

Peter had made a big impression on Felicity, it seemed. "Peter is a real smart boy," she said to me. "It's a pity he's a hired boy."

The passing of summer was scarcely noticed as we had so much fun together. Every evening the old orchard rang with laughter and squeals as we teased the girls.

"Bless the children," said Uncle Alec, as he carried the milk pails across the yard, his anger already forgotten. "Bless their hearts. Nothing can quench their fun." Little did he know that our fun would soon be quenched before too many days had passed.

Bitter Apples

Felix's opening move was a hard punch to Peter's right eye. It later turned black and blue and was quite painful. Peter punched back, and Felix's nose began to bleed.

Chapter Four

could never understand why my brother, Felix, was so upset about Peter winning the bitter-apple-eating contest, but he really took it to heart. Maybe it was because Peter had preached such a good sermon and we all knew he would have won if Sara Ray hadn't become hysterical. Or perhaps Felix just wanted to win some contest, any contest, I don't know.

But suddenly we all noticed that Felix just wasn't himself. He didn't seem to get any joy out of anything. It seemed that all he thought about or dreamed about was being able to eat one of the bitter apples without making a face. One night I heard him talking about it in his sleep. If anything could have made him thin, it would have been worrying over the bitter-apple-eating contest.

As for me, I could have cared less about the bitter apples. I had wanted to be successful in the sermon contest, and I felt bad every time I thought about the way we had been forced to abandon the competition. But I had no burning desire to eat sour apples without making a face. *Who cares?* I thought, and I couldn't sympathize with Felix. When I found out he was praying about it, I thought it was funny and told him so. But secretly I had hoped he would be able to do it since he wanted to so badly.

After three nights of praying, Felix managed to eat a bitter apple down to the next-to-the-last bite. But he couldn't finish it without making a face, no matter how hard he tried. At least he seemed a little encouraged that he could almost do it.

"Another prayer or two, and I'll be able to eat a whole apple," he said happily.

But that never happened, in spite of his prayers and efforts. Felix could never get beyond that last bite. For a time, this baffled him. But he felt the mystery was solved when Cecily told him that Peter was praying against him.

"He's praying that you'll never be able to eat a bitter apple without making a face," she said. "He told Felicity and Felicity told me. She said she thought it was real cute of him. But I think it's a dreadful way to talk about praying, and I told her so. She wanted me to promise not to tell you, but I wouldn't promise. I think it's fair for you to know what's going on."

Felix was very upset. "I don't see why God should answer Peter's prayers instead of mine," he said bitterly. "I've gone to church and Sunday school all my life, and Peter never went 'til this summer. It isn't fair."

"Oh, Felix, don't talk like that," said Cecily, shocked. "God is always fair. I'll tell you what I believe is the reason. Peter prays three times a day every day: in the morning, at lunch, and at night. Besides that, he prays any time he happens to think about it throughout the day. Maybe that's why his prayers are being answered. He's just praying more than you."

"I don't care how much he prays," said Felix. "It's not right that he prays against me. I won't put up with it, and I'll go and tell him so," he said firmly.

Felix marched over to Uncle Roger's with all of us trailing behind him, full of curiosity. We found Peter shelling beans in the barn, whistling as he worked.

"Look here, Peter," said Felix, "they've been telling me that you've been praying that I couldn't eat a bitter apple. Now I don't think that—"

"I never did!" exclaimed Peter. "I never mentioned your name. I never prayed that you couldn't eat a bitter apple. I just prayed that I'd be the only one who could."

"Well, that's the same thing," cried Felix. "You've just been praying that to spite me. And you've got to stop it, Peter Craig."

"Well, I just guess I won't," snapped Peter angrily. "I've as much right to pray for what I want as you,

Felix King, even if you were brought up in Toronto. I s'pose you think a hired boy hasn't any business praying for particular things, but I'll show you. I'll pray for what I please, and I'd like to see you try and stop me."

"You'll have to fight me if you keep on praying against me," said Felix.

The girls gasped, but Dan and I were happy. We hadn't seen a good fight for a long time.

"All right, I can fight as well as pray," agreed Peter.

"Oh, don't fight," begged Cecily. "That would be dreadful. Surely you can work it out some other way. Let's all give up the bitter apple contest. There isn't much fun in it. What does it matter?"

"I don't want to give it up," said Felix, "and I won't."

"Well, settle it some other way than fighting," insisted Cecily.

"I'm not wanting to fight," said Peter. "It's Felix. If he doesn't interfere with my praying, there's no need to fight. But if he does, there's no other way to settle it."

"But how will that settle it?" asked Cecily.

"Oh, whoever loses will have to give in about the praying," said Peter. "That's fair enough. If I lose I won't pray about the bitter apples anymore."

"It's awful to fight about praying," sighed poor Cecily.

"Aw, they were always fighting about religious things in the old days," said Felix. "The more religious something was the more fighting there was about it."

"A fellow's got a right to pray as he pleases," said Peter, "and if anybody tries to stop me, I'm bound to fight. That's my way of looking at it."

"What would Miss Marwood say if she knew you were going to fight?" asked Felicity.

Miss Marwood was our pastor's daughter and also Felix's Sunday school teacher. She was very pretty, and Felix was fond of her. Felicity hoped that by mentioning her, Felix wouldn't fight. But by that time, he was mad and quite reckless.

"I don't care what she would say," retorted Felix.

Felicity tried another tactic to stop the fight.

"You'll be sure to get whipped if you fight with Peter. You're too fat to fight."

This made Felix as mad as fire, and after that nothing could prevent him from fighting Peter.

"Why don't you settle it by drawing straws," suggested Cecily in desperation. "Whoever draws the shortest straw wins."

"That's just like gambling," stated Dan. "That's more wicked than fighting."

"What would your Aunt Jane say if she knew you were going to fight?" Cecily asked Peter.

"You leave my Aunt Jane out of this," snapped Peter.

"You said you were going to be a Presbyterian," tried Cecily again. "Good Presbyterians don't fight."

"Oh, don't they! I heard your uncle Roger say that Presbyterians were known for fighting—the best in the world—or the worst. I can't remember which he said, but it means the same thing."

"I thought you said in your sermon, *Master Peter,* that people shouldn't fight," said Felicity.

"I meant that they shouldn't fight for fun or sport. This is different. I know what I'm fighting for, but I can't think of the word."

"I guess you mean 'principle,'" I suggested.

"Yes, that's it," agreed Peter. "It's all right to fight for what you believe in. I believe I should be able to pray for what I want. And nothing can stop me," insisted Peter.

"Oh, can't you do something to stop them from fighting, Sara?" Cecily asked the Story Girl. Sara Stanley was sitting on the fence, swinging her shapely bare feet back and forth.

"It's not my place to meddle in the affairs of the boys," said the Story Girl.

If I'm not mistaken, I believe the Story Girl didn't mind that they were going to fight. She felt

It *was* kind of exciting. It was quickly arranged that the fight would take place in the pine woods behind Uncle Roger's barn. It was a dark private place, where grown-ups were unlikely to show up and stop them. The fight would take place at sunset.

"I hope Felix wins," said the Story Girl as we walked toward the woods that evening. "Not just for family honor, but because that was mean of Peter to pray that prayer. Do you think he will win?"

"I don't know," I confessed. "Felix is too fat, so he'll get out of breath in no time. Peter is cool, and he's a year older than Felix. On the other hand, Felix has had a little practice fighting some tough fellows in Toronto. This is Peter's first fight, so he's not as experienced."

"Did you ever fight?" the Story Girl asked me.

"Once," I answered shortly, dreading the next question.

"Who won?"

It's sometimes a terrible thing to have to tell the truth, especially to a young lady you greatly admire. I had a strong temptation to lie until I remembered that I had promised God on "Judgment Sunday" that I wouldn't do that anymore.

"The other fellow won," I said, although I hated to admit it.

"Well, it doesn't matter whether you get whipped or not, as long as you fight a good square fight."

Her answer made me feel that I was quite a hero after all. Somehow, her words took the sting out of the remembrance of that old fight.

When we arrived behind the barn, the others were all there. Cecily was very pale, and Felix and Peter were taking off their coats. There was a faded yellow sunset, and the pine wood was flooded with late-evening sunshine. A cool autumn wind was whistling among the branches, scattering red maple leaves all around us.

"Now," said Dan, "I'll count, and when I say 'three,' you go at each other until one of you has had enough. Cecily, keep quiet. Now one . . . two . . . three!"

Felix's opening move was a hard punch to Peter's right eye. It later turned black and blue and was quite painful. Peter punched back, and Felix's nose began to bleed. At the sight of blood, Cecily gave a shriek and ran out of the woods. We weren't sorry. Her disapproval was spoiling the fight for the rest of us.

After the first round of punches, the boys drew apart and circled each other. Just when they were locked in a wrestle with each other again, Uncle Alec walked around the corner of the barn. Cecily was behind him.

Uncle Alec wasn't angry. But there was a strange look in his eyes. He took hold of the fighters by their shirt collars and dragged them apart.

"This stops right here, boys," he said. "You know I don't allow fighting."

"Oh, but Uncle Alec, it was this way," began Felix eagerly. "Peter—"

"No, I don't want to hear about it," said Uncle Alec sternly. "I don't care what you were fighting about, but you must settle your quarrels in a different way. Remember what I say, Felix. Peter, Roger is looking for you to wash his buggy. Get going!"

Peter went off in a pout, and Felix sat down exhausted and began to mop up his bleeding nose. He turned his back to Cecily, obviously displeased that she had tattled on them to Uncle Alec.

Cecily caught it after Uncle Alec left. Dan called her a tattletale and a baby and sneered at her until she began to cry.

"I couldn't stand by and watch Felix and Peter pound each other all to pieces," she sobbed. "They've been great friends, and it was awful to see them fighting."

"Uncle Roger would have let them fight it out," said the Story Girl. "He believes in boys fighting. He says it's a harmless way for them to work out their anger. Peter and Felix would have been better friends if they had fought. Now the praying question won't be settled, unless Felicity can coax Peter to give up praying against Felix."

Felicity didn't like what the Story Girl said about her getting Peter to give up praying. She never would let on that she had any influence over him, but we knew she did.

"I don't meddle with *hired boys'* prayers," she said snootily.

"It's all nonsense anyway," said Dan. Now that there was to be no fight, he decided to let his real feelings show. "It was all nonsense in the first place, praying about the bitter apples."

"Oh, Dan, don't you believe there is some good in praying?" asked Cecily anxiously.

"Yes, I believe in praying but not in that way," said Dan sturdily. "I don't believe God cares whether anybody can eat an apple without making a face or not."

"You aren't well enough acquainted with God to know what prayers he will answer," said Felicity. She saw this as a good chance to snub her brother.

"There's something wrong here," said Cecily. "We ought to be able to pray for what we want. The Bible says that. And Peter wanted to be the only one who could pass the bitter apple test. I wish I could understand it all better."

"Peter's prayer was wrong because it was a self-ish prayer, I guess," said the Story Girl thoughtfully.

"Felix's prayer wouldn't have hurt anyone else, but it was selfish of Peter to want to be the only one. We shouldn't pray selfish prayers."

"Oh, I see through it now," cried Cecily joyfully.

"Yes, but you have to admit that God answered Peter's prayer.

A sharp wind blew around the barn and Cecily shivered. We heard Aunt Janet's voice calling, "Children, children." Shaking off the discussion of hired boy's prayers, we scrambled to our feet and hurried to our homes.

"Isn't it cold?" said Cecily, shivering again. "It will soon be winter. I wish it could always be summer. Felicity likes the winter and so does the Story Girl, but I don't. It always seems so long till spring."

"Never mind, we had a splendid summer," I said, slipping my arm about her to comfort her.

Truly, we had enjoyed a delicious summer and then the added time, which went well into fall; and it was ours forever.

Nevertheless, we all felt sad that our time together was coming to a close. We were sad until Felicity took us into the pantry and gave us luscious apple tarts and whipped cream. Then we brightened up. It was really a very decent world after all.

A Double Rainbow

What tales she told us on those glorious
autumn days. In her sparkling voice,
she made us imagine a beautiful princess
prancing through the orchard on her
white stallion or a gallant knight in
ruffled velvet riding for his lady.

Chapter Five

A s far as I can remember, Felix was never able to eat an entire bitter apple without making a face. He gave up trying after a while. He also gave up praying about it. He said there was no use praying about it when other fellows prayed against you out of spite. He and Peter were on bad terms for a long while.

We were all too tired during those nights in the fall to do any special praying. Sometimes I think our "regular" prayers were slurred or mumbled. I guess the Lord understands even when we don't. It was just that October was a busy month on the Island hill farms. The apples had to be harvested, and the work of picking them was mainly done by us children.

We stayed home from school to do it. That was acceptable to our teacher, as all the kids on the Island had to help or the harvest would have been lost. It was pleasant work and there was fun in it. But it was also hard work and our arms and backs ached at night. In the mornings, when we were rested, it was great. In the afternoons, it was bearable. But by evening when we were tired, we lagged, and there was not much fun in it at all.

Some of the apples had to be picked very carefully. Those were the very best ones that were to be sold. But with others (the ones to be used all winter for the family), it didn't matter so much. We boys would climb the trees and shake the apples down until the girls shrieked for mercy.

The days were crisp and mellow with warm sunshine and a tang of frost in the air. The smell of the old orchard was wonderful with the woodsy odors of withering grass and apples. The hens and turkeys prowled around, pecking at the "windfalls." That's what we called the apples that the winds blew down and left on the ground. Paddy rushed about chasing the chickens and turkeys in the fallen leaves. The world beyond the orchard was magnificent under the bright blue autumn sky.

The big willow tree, which our grandfather King had planted, was now displaying its glorious fall colors. The stately old tree spread its huge golden canopy skirt over us, providing cool shade during those warm days of autumn. The maple trees were also breathtaking in their blood-red beauty. Usually the Story Girl wound a crown of the red maple leaves around her head. She and the other girls looked beautiful as they stood on short ladders and picked apples.

Neither Felicity nor Cecily could have worn such a crown of leaves with the fall colors like the ones Sara Stanley wore. Their coloring was too pale for the brilliant wreaths she concocted. But when the Story Girl crowned her nut-brown hair with the crimson leaves and berries, she looked like a wood nymph. Peter said it looked like the wreaths grew on her.

What tales she told us on those glorious autumn days. In her sparkling voice, she made us imagine a beautiful princess prancing through the orchard on her white stallion or a gallant knight in ruffled velvet riding for his lady. Oh, those stories of long ago and the wonderful images of her characters that flitted through the old orchard.

When we had filled our apple baskets, they had to be carried to the barn loft and stored in bins or spread on the floor to ripen further. We ate a good many, of course, feeling it was payment for our work. The apples from our own "birthday trees" were stored in separate barrels with our names marked on each. We could do as we wished with them. Felicity sold hers to Uncle Alec's hired man. She got badly cheated in that deal as the hired man left before he had fully paid her. Felicity hasn't gotten over that to this day.

Our dear Cecily sent most of hers to the hospital in town and was rewarded by a good feeling of having done well with her little stash of wealth. The rest of us ate our apples or carried them to school. We traded them at school for other treasures our friends had that we wanted.

There was a dusky little pear-shaped apple, which came from one of Uncle Stephen's trees, that was our favorite. Next to that tree was another favorite— Aunt Louisa's delicious, juicy, yellow apple tree. We were really fond of those big sweet apples. We used to throw them up in the air and let them fall on the ground until they were bruised and bursting. Then we sucked the juice. To us it seemed as sweet as nectar from the gods.

Sometimes we worked until the cold yellow sunsets faded out into the dark distance beyond and the hunter's moon looked down on us through sparkling air. The constellations of stars in the autumn sky were gorgeous at night. I remember Peter standing on the Pulpit Stone one night before the moon rose, pointing them out to us. He and the Story Girl sometimes argued about the names of the stars, but Peter was truly amazing. He knew a lot more than a hired boy should be expected to know.

Some of the names of the constellations were known to all of us, such as the Big Dipper and the Little Dipper, but only Peter and the Story Girl knew the others. The names of these groups of stars rolled off their tongues as they educated us in astronomy.

Job's Coffin and the Northern Cross were to the west of us, where the waves of the blue Gulf rolled. Cassiopeia sat enthroned in her beautiful chair in the northeast. The Dippers swung themselves around the Pole Star. The Story Girl told us the myths and legends about these clusters of stars in a clear, remote, starry voice. When she ended each story, we came back to earth, feeling we had been a million miles away in the blue ethereal sky. All our old familiar surroundings were forgotten and strange for the moment.

That night, when Peter pointed out the stars to us from the Pulpit Stone, was the last time he shared our work and fun for several weeks. The next day he complained of a headache and a sore throat. He seemed to prefer lying on Aunt Olivia's kitchen sofa to doing any work. Peter was never known as a lazy guy, so we left him in peace while we picked apples—that is, all of us but Felix. He was still miffed at Peter about the bitter apple contest and spitefully declared that Peter was shirking his duties.

"He's just lazy, that's what's the matter with him," he said.

"If you have to talk, why don't you talk sense?" said Felicity angrily. "There's no reason to call Peter lazy. You might as well say I have black hair. Of course, Peter is a Craig and has his faults. But he's a smart boy. His father is lazy, but his mother doesn't have a lazy bone in her body. Peter takes after her."

"Uncle Roger says Peter's father isn't exactly lazy," said the Story Girl. "The trouble is that there are so many other things he likes better than work."

"I wonder if his father will ever come back to his family," said Cecily sadly. "Just think how dreadful it would be if *our* father had left us like that."

"Our father is a King," said Felicity proudly, "and Peter's father is only a Craig. A member of our family *couldn't* behave like that."

"They say there's a black sheep in every family," said the Story Girl.

"There isn't one in ours," said Cecily loyally.

"Why do white sheep eat more than black?" asked Felix.

"Is that a conundrum?" asked Cecily cautiously.

"What's a 'conundrum'?" I asked. I really didn't know.

"It's a riddle, silly," answered Felicity scornfully. "I would think a boy from *Toronto* would know." Felicity always seemed to know everything, and if she didn't she wouldn't admit it.

"Well, I can never guess *riddles* either," stated our honest cousin, Cecily.

"It isn't a riddle," said Felix. "It's a fact. Cross my heart. White sheep eat more than black sheep, and there's a good reason for it."

We stopped picking apples, sat down on the grass, and tried to reason it out. All of us, that is, except Dan. He declared he knew that there was a catch somewhere, and he wasn't going to be caught. The rest of us could not see where any catch could exist, especially since Felix had "crossed his heart" that it was true. We argued over it but finally conceded that we didn't know.

"Well, what is the reason?" demanded Felicity.

"Because there's more of them," said Felix, grinning from ear to ear. I forget what we did to him for his joke on us.

A shower came up in the evening, and we had to stop picking. After the rain there was a magnificent double rainbow. We watched it from the barn window

As the rainbow faded from our sky, the darkness of the October dusk was falling around us.

"Anytime I see a rainbow I think of God's promise that He will never destroy the earth again by a flood," Dan said. "What do you think a double rainbow means?"

"Maybe it's a promise that those who see it will live forever," said the Story Girl. "

"What do you think it would be like to live forever in this world?" he questioned.

"I expect we'd get tired of it after a while," said Story Girl.

"Oh, I don't think so," said Cecily. "Those who know God will live forever and I don't think we'll ever get tired of Heaven. Do you?"

We walked home thoughtfully in the quiet stillness of the October night.

The Shadow
Feared By Man

*At first Felicity looked away with her
snooty little nose in the air. But somehow,
she couldn't pretend anymore in the face of
death. "I guess . . . I do care for him," she
admitted, "but now he'll never know. He'll
die without knowing." And she broke into
fresh sobbing and wouldn't be comforted.*

Chapter Six

The next morning we apple pickers were all up early, dressing by candlelight. When we got downstairs, we were surprised to see the Story Girl had already come over to our house. Breakfast wasn't ready yet, but there she sat on Rachel Ward's blue chest. She looked very important, like she had big news. She did!

"What do you think?" she exclaimed. "Peter has the measles! He was dreadfully sick all night, and Uncle Roger had to go for the doctor. Peter was so dizzy and light-headed that he didn't know any of us. Of course he's far too sick to go home to his mother, so she has come up to Aunt Olivia's to take care of him. Aunt Olivia says I should live over here until he is better, so I won't catch them too."

This was bad news and good news. We were sorry to hear that Peter had the measles. But it would be fun to have the Story Girl living with us. What a time of storytelling we would have!

"I suppose we'll all have the measles now," grumbled Felicity. "And October is such an inconvenient time for illness. There is so much work to be done."

"I don't believe any time is very convenient to have the measles," Cecily said.

"Oh, perhaps we won't have them," said the Story Girl cheerfully. "Peter's mother says he caught them at Markdale the last time he was home."

"I don't want to catch the measles from Peter," Felicity said in a snooty tone. "Imagine catching them from a *hired boy!*"

"Please don't call Peter a hired boy when he's sick," protested Cecily.

During the next two days, we were very busy, really too busy to tell tales or listen to them. Only in the frosty dusk did we have time to hear Sara Stanley's tales. She had found a couple of old books of classic myths and northland folk stories in Aunt Olivia's attic. Each evening she told these stories that seemed so real that the elves and fairies and trolls jumped around the apple trees and played peekaboo with us in our imaginations.

On the third day she was living at our house, the Story Girl made her usual visit to Aunt Olivia's and knocked on the back porch door. She always wanted to find out each day how Peter was doing. She returned to our house with a white face. It was very obvious that she had bad news.

"Peter is very, very sick," she said miserably. "He has caught cold someway . . . and the measles have 'struck in,' whatever that means." The Story Girl wrung her tanned hands. "The doctor is . . . is afraid . . . he . . . won't get . . . better."

We all stood around staring at her. It was impossible!

"Do . . . do you mean that . . . Pete . . . is going to . . . die?" asked Felix, finding his voice at last.

The Story Girl nodded her head miserably. "They're afraid so."

Cecily sat down by her half-filled basket of apples and began to cry. Felicity said violently that she didn't believe it.

"I can't pick another apple today, and I ain't going to try," said Dan.

None of us could bear to work. We went to the grown-ups and told them so. They told us we didn't have to. They felt as bad as we did. We kids wandered around like little lost souls trying to comfort one another. We steered clear of the orchard. It was too full of happy memories for us to go there. Instead we went to the spruce woods, where the hush and the soft sighing of the wind in the branches didn't jar on our new sorrow.

We couldn't believe that Peter was going to die— to *die!* To us, old people died, grown-up people died, even children we knew died. But it wasn't possible that one of *us* could die. It just wasn't possible. And yet the possibility was staring us in the face.

We sat on the mossy stones under dark evergreen trees and gave in to our tears. All of us, even Dan, cried. All, that is, except the Story Girl.

"I don't see how you can be so unfeeling, Sara Stanley," rebuked Felicity. "You've always been such good friends with Peter and have always stuck up for him. Now you haven't shed even one tear for him."

"I can't cry," Sara said drearily. "I wish I could. I've a dreadful feeling here," she touched her slender throat. "And if I could cry, I think it would make it better. But I can't."

"Maybe Peter will get better after all," said Dan, swallowing a sob. "I've heard of lots of people getting better after the doctor said they'd die."

"Well, 'As long as there's life, there's hope,' you know," said Felix. "We shouldn't cross bridges till we come to them."

"Those are only old sayings," said the Story Girl bitterly. "They are all very fine when there's nothing to worry you, but when you're in real trouble, they're not a bit of help."

"Oh, I wish I'd never said Peter wasn't fit to associate with us," moaned Felicity. "If he'd just get better, I'll never say such a thing again. I'll never even *think* it. He's just a lovely boy and twice as smart as lots of boys who aren't hired out."

"He's always been so polite and good-natured," sighed Cecily.

"He was just a real gentleman," said the Story Girl. "I shouldn't say 'was.' I should say 'is.' He isn't dead yet."

"What's the difference? He's almost gone from us. There ain't many fellows as fair and square as Peter," said Dan sadly.

"It's too late to be saying all these nice things about him now," said the Story Girl. "He won't ever know how much we thought of him. It's too late."

"I wish I hadn't boxed his ears the time he tried to kiss me," Felicity went on. She was taking it very hard, so hard that I wondered if her conscience was bothering her. "Of course I couldn't be expected to let a hir ... to let a boy kiss me. But I needn't have been so cross about it. I might have been more dignified. And I told him I just *hated* him." Felicity's beautiful blue eyes swam with tears.

"I never thought you hated him," said the Story Girl practically. "I thought you had a crush on him. But it's hard to tell what he thought you thought of him."

At first Felicity looked away with her snooty little nose in the air. But somehow, she couldn't pretend anymore in the face of death. "I guess ... I do care for him," she admitted, "but now he'll never know. He'll die without knowing." And she broke into fresh sobbing and wouldn't be comforted.

"Oh, it's awful," said Sara Stanley. "What makes people say and do such awful things? If we only knew the future, we'd surely be more careful with our words." All of us nodded our heads in agreement.

"Yeah, but if we knew the future, how could we stand it?" I asked. "I think God is merciful not to let us know. Then we can be happy until it happens."

"I suppose that if Peter d–d–dies he'll go to heaven. But you never know," sobbed Cecily. "He isn't a church member yet, although he's been real good all summer."

"I don't think being good is what counts," said the Story Girl wisely.

"He's a Presbyterian, you know," said Felicity, as if that made all the difference. She acted as though being a Presbyterian swung the gates of heaven wide open.

"Being a Presbyterian or Baptist or whatever isn't what makes the difference. It's what you believe," stated Cecily simply.

"He couldn't go to the bad place, could he?" asked Felix. "I mean what would they do with him there, when he's so good and polite and all?"

"It isn't what you do that gets you to heaven," said the Story Girl. "I think you have to believe right."

84

"I'm pretty sure he believes right, but he never went to church much and maybe he doesn't know what's right," stated Cecily.

"It sure is hard to know," sighed Felix. "But Peter did read the Bible a lot, 'specially when he was gettin' his sermon ready. I have to admit, he really won that contest. I mean he sure preached hard against the bad place. And he would have made sure he wouldn't go there."

"Oh, I think he'll be all right too," answered Cecily. "It's not his fault that his father ran away, and his mother was too busy earning a living to bring him up right."

"Don't forget his Aunt Jane helped him a lot and gave him that Bible. He'll go to heaven, I think. But I don't want him to go—at least not yet. I want him to stay right here with us. I know heaven is a wonderful place, but I'm sure Peter isn't anxious to go and leave all the fun we have here," said the Story Girl.

"Sara Stanley! I'm ashamed of you for saying such things at a time like this," ranted Felicity.

"Well, wouldn't you rather be here yourself than in heaven right now?" answered the Story Girl bluntly. "Wouldn't you now, Felicity King? Tell the truth—cross your heart."

Felicity's answer was only another outburst of tears.

"If we could only do something to help Peter!" I said desperately. "It seems dreadful not to be able to do a single thing."

"There's one thing we can do," said Cecily gently. "We can pray for him."

"That's right!" Dan said, brightening up. Quite a mouthful for Dan who never seemed very excited about prayer.

"I'm going to pray real hard," said Felix with new hope.

All of us agreed. There was something we could do. It was good news.

"We'll have to be awful good, you know," warned Cecily. "There's no use in praying if you're not good."

"That will be easy," sighed Felicity. "I don't feel a bit like being bad. If anything happens to Peter, I feel sure I'll never be naughty again. I won't have the heart."

We did indeed pray constantly for Peter's recovery. We didn't, as in the case of Paddy, just tack it on after more important things, but it was the topic that had all of our attention. Dan's doubt and lack of faith fell away like an old coat no longer needed. The "valley of the shadow of death," which sifts and tries our souls, was upon us. We grew up overnight with the weight of the possibility of losing our beloved Peter. Even the grown-ups came to a new realization of how puny their faith was. We all came crawling humbly to the God we thought we could do without. Now in our deep need, we were each to find his strength for our weakness.

The hours of prayer seemed to have no effect. Peter was no better the next day. Aunt Olivia reported that his mother was brokenhearted. We didn't ask the grown-ups to release us from work. Instead we went back to work with feverish zeal. We felt that if we worked hard, there would be less time for grief and morbid thoughts of death.

We picked apples and dragged them to the barn loft. In the afternoon, Aunt Janet brought us out a lunch of apple turnovers, but we couldn't eat them. All of us remembered how much Peter loved apple turnovers. There was no fun about anything. Our only thought was for our friend.

"Oh, I would make a hundred turnovers for him if he would only get well," said Felicity.

She truly seemed changed. Her pride didn't show. She had been humbled by having to call on God and beg for mercy for Peter.

Oh, how good we were! How angelic and unnaturally well behaved! Never was there such a band of kind, sweet-tempered, unselfish children in any orchard. Even Felicity and Dan got through the days without arguments.

When evening came, we went to the orchard to talk and try to comfort each other. It was a beautiful night—clear, windless, and frosty. Someone galloped down the road on horseback, loudly singing a comic song. How dare he! We felt that if we were miserable, the whole world should be.

Sometime later Aunt Olivia came down the grassy path in the twilight. Her bright hair was uncovered, and she looked slim and queenlike in her light dress. We thought Aunt Olivia was very pretty. That night she looked beautiful in the autumn dusk as she stood in front of us, smiling at our sad faces.

"Dear little sorrowful people, I have some good news. The doctor has just been here, and he thinks Peter is much better. There is a very good chance he may pull through after all."

We looked up at her in stunned silence for a few moments. It was almost more than we could comprehend. Just a few weeks before, we had been happy and noisy when we learned that Paddy was going to recover. But now we were quiet. We had been too near something dark and terrible. To understand that the threat of death was removed was almost too much for us.

The Story Girl, who had been standing up leaning against a pine tree, slipped down to the ground in a huddle and began to weep with a passion. I had never heard anyone cry so hard before. I was used to hearing girls cry. Sara Ray, of course, cried nearly every day. Even Cecily and Felicity cried often. But none of them had cried like this. I felt the same as I had the time I saw my father cry. It was a strange feeling.

"Oh, don't, Sara, don't," I said gently, patting her shaking shoulder.

"You are a strange girl," said Felicity. "You never cried a speck when you thought Peter was going to die, and now when he is going to get better, you cry like that."

"Sara dear, come with me," said Aunt Olivia, bending over her. The Story Girl got up and Aunt Olivia put her arm around Sara's shoulders. The sound of her crying died away as they left the orchard. With their leaving, our dread and grief seemed to vanish also. Suddenly we were all happy as clams.

"Oh, ain't it great that Peter's going to be all right?" said Dan, springing up on his feet.

"I was never so glad of anything in my whole life," declared Felicity happily.

"Can't we send word somehow to Sara Ray tonight?" asked Cecily, who was always thoughtful. "She's feeling so bad, and she'll feel that way all night unless we can tell her."

"Let's all go down to the Ray gate and holler to Judy Pineau till she comes out," suggested Felix.

Accordingly, we went and hollered loudly. We were much surprised when Sara's mother came to the gate instead of Judy. She rather sourly demanded to know what we were yelling about. When she heard our news, however, she had the decency to say she was glad and to promise she would tell Sara right away. "Sara is already in bed, where all children of her age should be," she added severely.

We had no intention of going to bed for a good two hours yet. We walked back up the hill, thanking the Lord that our grown-ups were not like Mrs. Ray. All of us went to the barn and lit a huge lantern that Dan had made from a pumpkin. We devoured as many apples as we wanted and celebrated that our dear Peter would not be taken from us. By the light of our goblin lantern, our faces were shining with joy. Life was happy once again.

"I'm going to make a big batch of raspberry tarts first thing in the morning," said Felicity. "Maybe Peter will be able to eat one. He likes them so much. Isn't it funny? Last night none of us wanted to do anything but pray. Tonight I just feel like cooking and singing."

"We mustn't forget to thank God for making Peter better," said Cecily, as we went into the house.

"Don't you s'pose Peter would have gotten better anyway?" asked Dan.

"Oh, Dan, what makes you ask such questions?" exclaimed Cecily in disappointment.

"I dunno," said Dan. "They just kind of come into my head. But, of course, I mean to thank God when I say my prayers tonight. That's only decent."

"Well, I should hope you would," Felix said.

He got total agreement from all of us on that statement.

We Hear from Peter

Perhaps I'd never have realized what good friends I have if the measles hadn't struck in. I guess having the measles isn't too bad if you can learn some things you never knew. So I'm glad they struck in, but I hope they never will again.

Chapter Seven

nce Peter was out of danger, he recovered rapidly but found it tedious having to stay in bed. He was lonely and missed all of us. Aunt Olivia suggested one day that we write letters to amuse him until he was well enough to come to the window and talk. Since it was Saturday and the apples had been picked, we took off for the orchard to write our letters.

In Felicity's letter to Peter she told him she felt terrible when she heard he might die. She admitted to him that she really did like him a lot. In fact, she told him she thought she loved him.

I think her letter to him helped him recover more quickly than anything else. Peter was glad to receive all of our letters and insisted on answering them himself. Aunt Olivia wrote his to us just as he dictated it. Well, all that is except the mistakes in grammar and spelling. He said he would be glad to have his sickness over because the castor oil was so bad it would "make a pig puke." He thanked us all for praying for him, especially Cecily, and said he couldn't wait to see Felicity again.

We all rolled our eyes at each other when we read that. It was no doubt he and Felicity were "sweet" on each other. I will let you read one of his letters back to us.

I'm glad you are still praying for me, Cecily, for you can't trust the measles. They might strike in at any minute. And I would sure be embarrassed to die of them. It just doesn't seem manly to die of the measles. Anyway, keep up the praying—so far it's worked good for cats and boys. Cecily I would like to borrow that little red book of yours, The Safe Compass. It's such a good book to read on Sundays. It is interesting and religious too.

So is the Bible. I hadn't quite finished the Bible yet when I got the measles. Ma is reading the last chapters to me. It gets real exciting at the end, with lots of terrible stuff going on. I'm glad I won't be here on earth when it all happens. Since I was so sick, I made sure I know where I'm going when I die. There's an awful lot in the Bible to think about. I can't understand the whole of it, since I'm only a hired boy, but some parts are real easy. I mean to get me an educa-

tion when I get older to learn more about a lot of things. Then I won't just be a hired boy.

I'm awful glad you all have such a good opinion of me. I don't deserve it, but after this I'll try to. I can't tell you how I feel about all your kindness.

Felix, I've given up praying that I'd be the only one to eat the bitter apples, and I'll never pray for anything selfish like that again. It was a horrid, mean prayer. Anyhow, all the letters were fine. I'm awful glad I have so many nice friends, even if I am only a hired boy. Perhaps I'd never have realized what good friends I have if the measles hadn't struck in. I guess having the measles isn't too bad if you can learn some things you never knew. So I'm glad they struck in, but I hope they never will again.

Your loyal friend,
Peter Craig

November's Dream

The next morning, November wakened
from her dream of May in a bad temper.
A cold autumn rain set in that reminded us
that winter was just around the corner.

Chapter Eight

We celebrated the November day when Peter was able to rejoin us by having a picnic in the orchard. Sara Ray was also allowed to come, and her joy in being with us again was almost pitiful. She and Cecily cried in one another's arms as if they had been apart for years.

It was a beautiful day for our picnic. November dreamed that it was May. The air was soft and mellow, and the leafless trees on the western hills could have been awaiting buds rather than preparing for winter. It was a farewell party for the glorious summer as our orchard prepared for its winter sleep.

"It's just like spring, isn't it?" said Felicity.

"No, not quite. It looks like spring, but it isn't," the Story Girl said. "It's as if everything is resting—getting ready to sleep. In spring everything is getting ready to grow. Can't you *feel the difference?*"

"I think it's just like spring," insisted Felicity, running her fingers through her hair. She was pretty, but she didn't have much imagination.

In the sun-sweet place in front of the Pulpit Stone, we boys had put up a board table. Aunt Janet allowed us to cover it with an old tablecloth. The girls artfully covered the worn places in the old cloth with frost-whitened ferns and lovely colored leaves.

We used the kitchen dishes, and the centerpiece was Cecily's three geraniums and maple leaves in the cherry vase. As for the food, it was exquisite. Felicity had outdone herself. She had spent nearly two days preparing food "fit for a King," even though the party was in honor of our dear hired boy, Peter, who was not a King but only a Craig. There was no doubt now that Felicity *liked* Peter, but the Craig name was hard for her to take. Her pride was still in the way but not quite like it was before Peter's near-death illness.

Her crowning achievement was a rich, little plum cake with white frosting. On it was "Welcome Back" lettered in pink candies. Peter was nearly overcome when she placed it daintily in front of him.

"To think that you'd go to so much trouble for me!" he said with an adoring look at Felicity. She got all the gratitude and credit, although the Story Girl had come up with the whole idea, seeded the raisins, and beaten the eggs. Cecily had trudged all the way to Mrs. Jameson's little shop below the church to buy the pink candies. But isn't that the way of the world?

"We ought to say grace," said Felicity as we sat down to eat. "Will anyone say it?"

She looked at me, but I blushed to the roots of my hair and shook my head sheepishly. An awkward silence fell. It looked as if we would have to get along without grace, even though all of us were thankful to have our Peter back with us. Suddenly Felix shut his eyes, bent his head, and prayed a very nice prayer without any embarrassment at all. We looked at him with new respect when he said amen.

"Where did you learn to pray like that, Felix?" I asked. We didn't usually have prayer before we ate in our home with Father.

"It's the grace Uncle Alec says at every meal," answered Felix.

We all felt rather ashamed of ourselves. Was it possible that we had paid so little attention to Uncle Alec's grace that we didn't recognize it?

"Now," said Felicity happily, "let's enjoy and eat everything all up."

She didn't need to tell us twice. We had gone without our dinners in order to "save our appetites" and did ample justice to Felicity's good things. Paddy sat on the Pulpit Stone and watched us with great yellow eyes. He knew tidbits would come his way later on. We had been saving jokes to tell Peter since we knew he was going to get well. We laughed and ate till we were nearly sick.

"My sides hurt from laughing," said Peter. We looked at him with alarm.

"Are you gonna be sick again?" asked Dan.

"No way!" assured Peter. "Now let's play some games." He was determined to make up for all the lost time from when he was sick.

The girls took things back to the house as we guys put the table boards away in the barn. Then the games began. Our favorite was hide-and-seek with no holds barred. Even the barn and the storage bins weren't off-limits. We whooped and hollered as we played until dusk and then went to the back field to burn the potato stalks. This was a fun thing to do in the Fall after the potatoes were dug and stored away for the winter. Uncle Alec was there to help us set fire to them—the crowning delight of the day.

In a few minutes, the field was alight with blazing bonfires, with great columns of smoke everywhere. We ran from pile to pile, poking each one with long sticks. The gushes of rose-red sparks streaming up into the night, the whirling of smoke and firelight, and the dancing shadows caused our imaginations to take flight.

After a while we grew tired of our sport and perched on the high pole fence that separated the field from the dark spruce woods. The wind made strange sounds as it blew through the trees behind us. The shadowy forms of our uncles tending the fires reminded us of Peter's sermon about the bad place.

"I'm glad Sara Ray isn't here now," said Cecily. "I know she was sad to go home early, but she wouldn't like it now. The fields look just like ... well, you know."

"They do look like what I think the bad place must be like," said the Story Girl. "I know a story about a man who once saw the devil."

"Oh, don't tell it, Sara," said Cecily with a shudder. "Remember what Mother said about telling terrible stories."

"Oh, well, she was talking about make-believe stories. This is a true story about a real man who—"

"I think it's best not to tell it, Story Girl," said Peter wisely. "There are some things that don't need to be told. Since I was so sick, I have a different thought about the ... the devil. I know he's real. I think he would like us to think about him and talk about him a lot so that we can scare each other. But he isn't worth talking about. There's no sense in it."

"Well, I guess you're right, Peter," agreed the Story Girl. "The young man I was going to tell you about didn't believe there was a devil."

"I'm not saying that," said Peter, shaking his head. "There certainly is a devil and he is our enemy. The Bible says so."

"William Cowan, the man the story is about, could have told you he is real," said the Story Girl. "William Cowan was a wild and wicked young man who laughed at people who went to church. He even laughed at the thought of the devil. He would just swagger around and say that if there were a devil, he liked him and wanted to go be with him."

"Oh," gasped Cecily. "He was in great danger of . . . of going to the bad place."

"I wouldn't have wanted to be in his shoes," replied Felix with wide eyes.

"Well, one summer evening, his mother pleaded with him to go to church with her, but he wouldn't. He said he was going fishing instead. When church time came, he marched past the church with his fishing rod over his shoulder, singing the worst song you could ever imagine.

"When asked where he was going, he said, 'I'm going to the devil. Wanna come with me?'

"I won't tell the rest of the story because it's pretty scary," said the Story Girl. "But that night as he walked past the old woods, just down the road from the church, he had an awful experience with the devil. People say that the devil fought with him and left a mark on his left shoulder."

"Tell us the rest," begged Dan. "How did he get the mark on him?"

"He would never say," answered the Story Girl, "but his hair turned white overnight. It changed his life forever. He never would talk about it. His only answer when asked what happened was, 'It made a believer out of me.' Indeed he did become a believer, and anytime the church doors were open, he was there. He became an elder in the church and was always one to help young people who were starting to go astray. People respected him highly because they knew what he had been through. He's buried in the churchyard in the Cowan plot," finished the Story Girl. "His stone has an open Bible on it and it says: 'Here lies beneath this sod / A true believer gone to God.'"

Even though the story had a good ending, we all had creepy feelings. The piles of potato stalks were still smoldering, and the shadows of the men tending them were still dancing around in the field. The wind was picking up, and the spruce trees were moaning behind us. Winter's chill was coming.

Fortunately Uncle Alec came along and said he thought we'd better go home since the fires were nearly out. We slid down from the fence and started to the house, taking care to keep close together. It was comforting to hear Uncle Alec's footsteps behind us. Beyond us the home light was glowing from the windows of the King farmhouse on the hill.

The next morning, November wakened from her dream of May in a bad temper. A cold autumn rain set in that reminded us that winter was just around the corner. Later that day, a freezing wind came up, and along with it a weak wintry sun peeped out. Felicity, the Story Girl, and I walked down to the post office for the mail. Felicity wore her new velvet hood with its little ruff of white fur. Her golden curls framed her lovely face and her cheeks were stung bright pink by the sharp wind. She was on my right. The Story Girl, her red cap on her sleek brown head, was on my left, scattering her words along the path as we walked. I remember we met some of the Carlisle boys, and I felt lucky to have such beauty and charm with me.

As we walked, we talked about the mail that might be waiting. "I hope there isn't a letter from Father saying that Felix and I must start for Toronto," I worried. "He surely will be coming back from South America soon and will want us to come home."

"Oh, Bev, you can't go yet," protested Felicity. "We're going to have such fun this winter."

"Even school is fun when we're all together," said the Story Girl. "Can't you get him to let you stay at least till Christmas?"

"If he comes back to Toronto, Felix and I will have to go," I said sadly. "We really miss Father and want to see him, but we'll miss being here too."

Sure enough, there was a thin letter from Father among the others. I took it from the box with dread as Felicity and the Story Girl claimed their own mail. Neither of them were paying much attention to me. If they had been, they would have noticed how my hands shook as I tore it open. I knew my question was about to be answered. The Story Girl was totally absorbed in a letter from her father postmarked from Paris, and Felicity was reading some silly note from a friend at school.

"Look!" I shouted, dancing about, waving my letter. "Father has been asked to stay another six months in the South American office. He sends a large check for us to buy gifts for the family for Christmas and will write to Uncle Alec with more details."

I was deliriously happy and so were the girls. We grabbed hands and danced around on the porch of the post office like fools. Anne Shirley, a cousin of ours from up at Green Gables, was working the post office. Amused, she watched us cavorting and then came out to congratulate us that Felix and I could stay in Avonlea awhile longer. "It's a very special place," she told us. Of course, we already knew that.

The Story Girl and Peter came over that night, and we made taffy in the kitchen.

While stirring the candy, the Story Girl said, "It's been a wonderful summer but now that it's over we can only imagine what the holiday and winter will be like."

"It's better to know than to imagine," said Felicity.

"Oh no, it isn't," said the Story Girl quickly. "When you know things, you have to go by facts.

But when you just dream about things, there's nothing to hold you down."

"You're letting the taffy scorch, and *that's* a fact you'd better go by," said Felicity, sniffing. "Haven't you got a nose?"

When we went to bed, the moon was making a fairyland of the snowy world outside. From where I lay, I could see the tops of the spruce trees against the silvery sky. The winds were still, and the land lay in beauty. Across the hall, the Story Girl, who was staying all night, was telling Felicity and Cecily an old tale. I wished I could hear it better, but they were whispering so the grown-ups couldn't hear.

Our summer had been a beautiful one, and now Felix and I could stay and enjoy fall too. As I drifted off to sleep, there was the pleasure of knowing I was among my family who were also my dearest friends. We had shared delightful days of hard work and the purple peace of carefree nights. We had shared the pleasure of bird songs and silver rain on the green fields and storms among the trees.

Now there was the promise of the winter to come, the joys of the holidays, and before we could imagine, there were the dreams of spring to tantalize us. It is always safe to dream of spring, for it is sure to come. And beyond it was our future—a mystery yet unopened. I agreed with the Story Girl. It is better to dream, for then there is nothing to hold you down.

Lucy Maud Montgomery
1908

Lucy Maud Montgomery
1874-1942

Anne of Green Gables was the very first book that Lucy Maud Montgomery published. In all, she wrote twenty-five books.

Lucy Maud Montgomery was born on Prince Edward Island. Her family called her Maud. Before she was two years old, her mother died and she was sent to live with her mother's parents on their farm on the Island. Her grandparents were elderly and very strict. Maud lived with them for a long time.

When she was seven, her father remarried. He moved far out west to Saskatchewan, Canada, with his new wife. At age seventeen, she went to live with them, but she did not get along with her stepmother. So she returned to her grandparents.

She attended college and studied to become a teacher—just like Anne in the Avonlea series. When her grandfather died, Maud went home to be with her grandmother. Living there in the quiet of Prince Edward Island, she had plenty of time to write. It was during this time that she wrote her first book, *Anne of Green Gables*. When the book was finally accepted, it was published soon after. It was an immediate hit, and Maud began to get thousands of letters asking for more stories about Anne. She wrote *Anne of Avonlea, Chronicles of Avonlea, Anne of the Island, Anne of Windy Poplars, Anne's House of Dreams, Rainbow Valley, Anne of Ingleside,* and *Rilla of Ingleside*. She also wrote *The Story Girl* and *The Golden Road*.

When Maud was thirty-seven years old, Ewan Macdonald, the minister of the local Presbyterian Church in Canvendish, proposed marriage to her. Maud accepted and they were married. Later on they moved to Ontario where two sons, Chester and Stewart, were born to the couple.

Maud never went back to Prince Edward Island to live again. But when she died in 1942, she was buried on the Island, near the house known as Green Gables.